This Walker book belongs to:

_____

_____

First published 1989 by Walker Books Ltd, 87 Vauxhall Walk, London SE11 5HJ

This edition published 2021

2 4 6 8 10 9 7 5 3 1

Text © 1989 John Yeoman
Illustrations © 1989 Quentin Blake

The right of John Yeoman and Quentin Blake to be identified as author and illustrator respectively
of this work has been asserted by them in accordance with the Copyright, Designs and Patents Act 1988

This book has been typeset in Bembo

Printed in China

British Library Cataloguing in Publication Data:
a catalogue record for this book is available from the British Library

ISBN 978-1-4063-9590-7

www.walker.co.uk

Old Mother Hubbard's Dog
Needs a Doctor

John Yeoman
Quentin Blake

WALKER BOOKS
AND SUBSIDIARIES
LONDON · BOSTON · SYDNEY · AUCKLAND

Said Old Mother Hubbard one fine afternoon,
Preparing to polish the bell,
"You ought to be taking some exercise soon:
You're really not looking too well."

And while she was dusting and sweeping the floor
And shining the pans and the pots,
The dog found some paint tins behind the back door
And covered himself in bright spots.

She made a strong soup, using carrots and peas
And turnips and onions and such,
Thinking, "This ought to cure him of any disease."
But the dog hopped away on a crutch.

He reappeared, causing his mistress to stare,
And tremble, and turn very pale:
He was bowling along in an invalid chair
And was bandaged from whiskers to tail.

He then had the hiccoughs, which frightened the cat,
And made all the window frames shake.
Said Old Mother Hubbard, "I'm not standing that:
My head is beginning to ache."

The dog looked quite sorry, and took to his bed;

She saw his tears starting to form.

She gave him a large block of ice for his head

And bedsocks to keep his feet warm.

She knew that there wasn't a moment to lose;
She saddled her pig in the sty.
She went for the doctor. He wouldn't refuse:
Her poor little dog mustn't die.

They trotted back slowly (the pig wouldn't run);
She felt much too anxious to talk.
But there was her dog, doing handsprings for fun,
Before setting off for a walk.

The Adventures of Old Mother Hubbard's Dog

Also illustrated by Quentin Blake

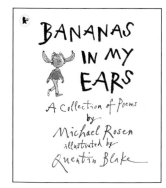

Available from all good booksellers